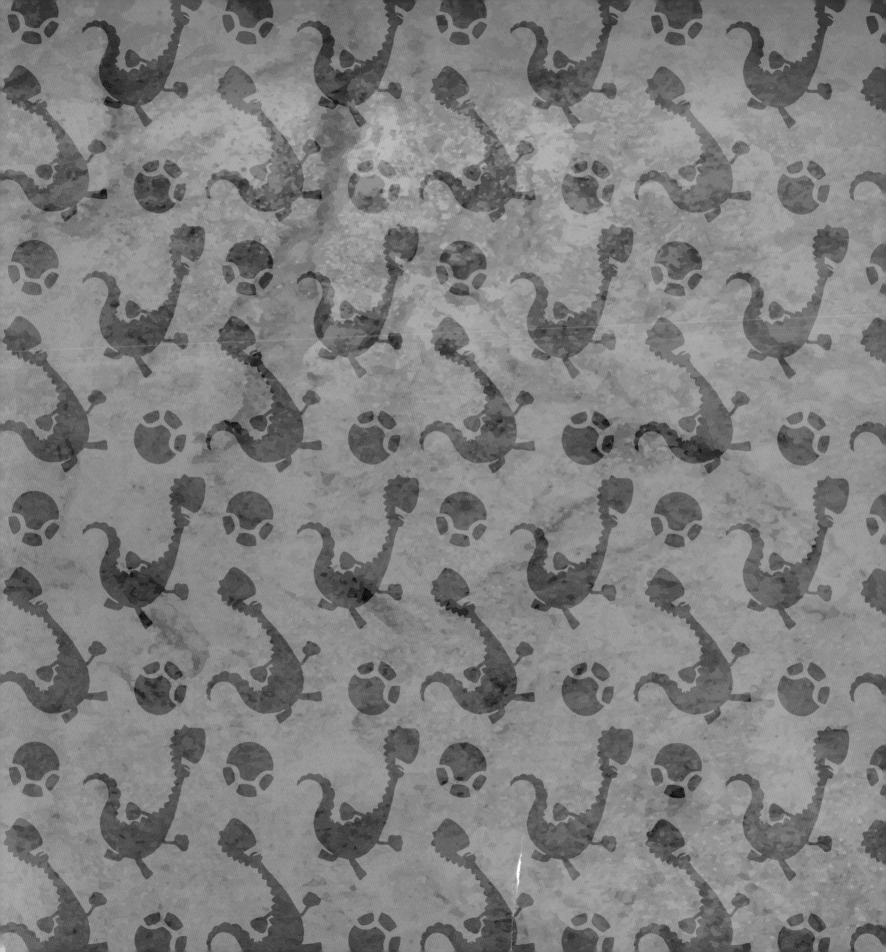

GIGANTOSAURUS™

Dream Big,
BILL

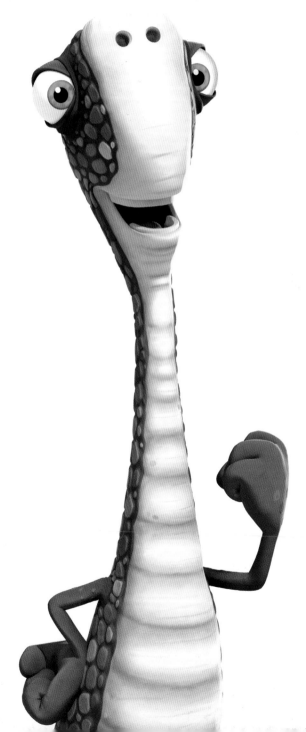

templar
books

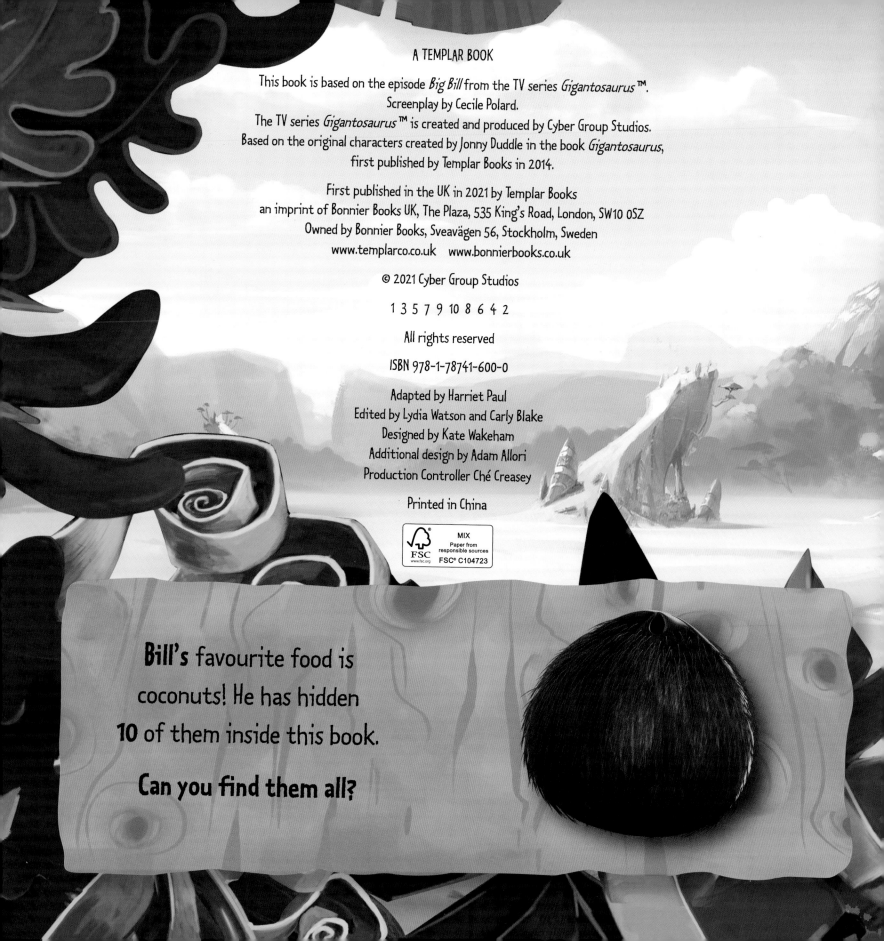

A TEMPLAR BOOK

This book is based on the episode *Big Bill* from the TV series *Gigantosaurus*™.
Screenplay by Cecile Polard.
The TV series *Gigantosaurus*™ is created and produced by Cyber Group Studios.
Based on the original characters created by Jonny Duddle in the book *Gigantosaurus*,
first published by Templar Books in 2014.

First published in the UK in 2021 by Templar Books
an imprint of Bonnier Books UK, The Plaza, 535 King's Road, London, SW10 0SZ
Owned by Bonnier Books, Sveavägen 56, Stockholm, Sweden
www.templarco.co.uk   www.bonnierbooks.co.uk

ISBN 978-1-78741-600-0

Adapted by Harriet Paul
Edited by Lydia Watson and Carly Blake
Designed by Kate Wakeham
Additional design by Adam Allori
Production Controller Ché Creasey

Printed in China

Bill's favourite food is coconuts! He has hidden 10 of them inside this book.

Can you find them all?

This story is all about **BILL**, the little blue brachiosaurus. Although Bill will grow up to be one of the BIGGEST dinos in Cretacia, for now he's the BIGGEST scaredy-saur. Here's how he learned that even the most fearsome dinosaur of all was once small (and scared) too . . .

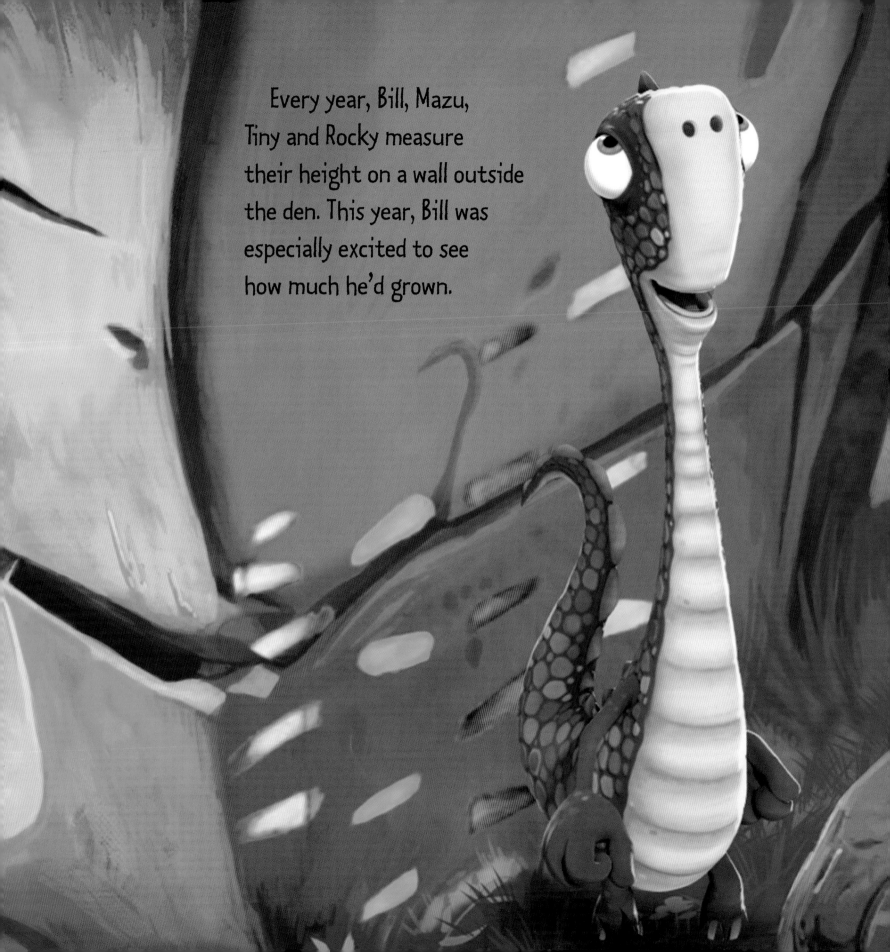

Every year, Bill, Mazu, Tiny and Rocky measure their height on a wall outside the den. This year, Bill was especially excited to see how much he'd grown.

Bill quickly ducked into the den to hide. He was scared of lots of things.
In fact, almost EVERYTHING! But the thing that terrified him
the most was GIGANTOSAURUS.

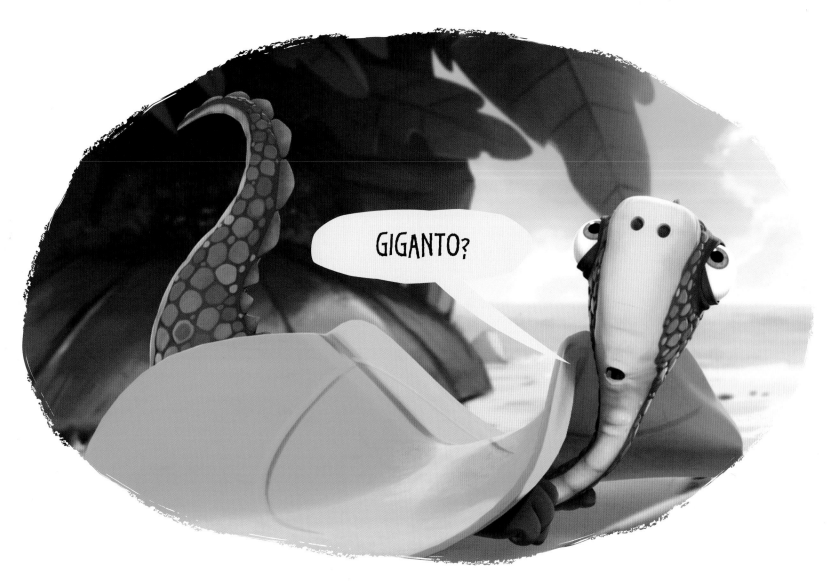

The little dino lay quivering under a leaf, until he heard
a familiar voice outside. It wasn't Giganto stomping around.
It was Ayati, the wise old brachiosaurus.

Ayati was always ready to listen to the little dinos, so Bill told her how frightened he was of Giganto.

"Some day when you're big like me, you won't be afraid," Ayati reassured him. "Why don't you come up here and see what it's like?"

At first, Bill was scared to be so high up, but he soon began to enjoy himself.

"Look at me!" he called, waving to his friends below. "I'm BIG!"

From his high viewpoint, Bill could see right across the savannah. Pterosaurs flew past him and he could see his herd grazing in the distance.

Back at the den, Tiny, Mazu and Rocky couldn't wait to hear all about Bill's ride with Ayati.

"It was amazing!" Bill told his friends excitedly. "I wasn't even scared of Giganto."

That's when Bill decided that he wanted to be big NOW. How could he grow big FAST?

Wise old Ayati had an idea. "There's a mysterious dinosaur in Cretacia who knows ALL the secrets to growing up," she told them.

Do you think you can find out who it is?

Bill didn't want to waste any time. Together, the little dinos raced off to start looking.

There was just one problem – they had no idea what the mystery dino looked like! Tiny pointed to a large, LEAFY-LOOKING dinosaur up ahead.

"Could that be the mystery dino?" she said.

Bill took a deep breath and tried to be brave as he approached.
"E-e-excuse me . . . are YOU the mystery dino?"

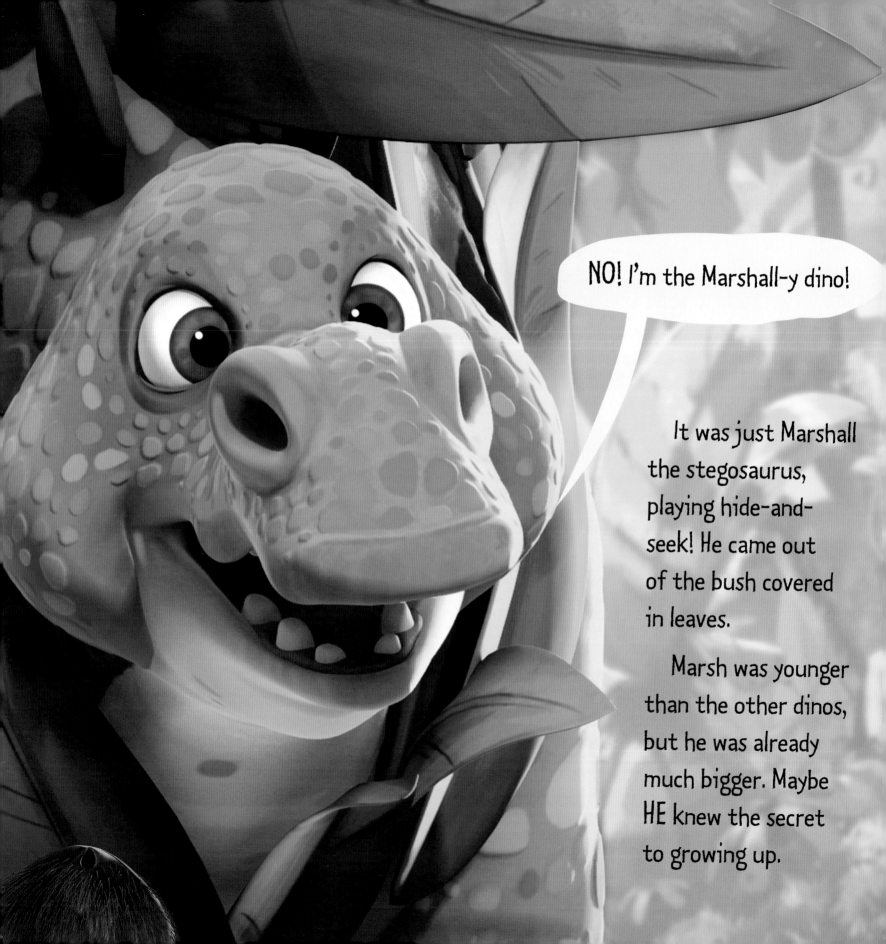

NO! I'm the Marshall-y dino!

It was just Marshall the stegosaurus, playing hide-and-seek! He came out of the bush covered in leaves.

Marsh was younger than the other dinos, but he was already much bigger. Maybe HE knew the secret to growing up.

Suddenly, Rugo the rat popped out of her underground tunnel right in front of them. Marsh squealed in fright and leapt into Bill's arms!

Bill was surprised. "How can a BIG dino like you be scared of something as SMALL as Rugo?" he asked Marsh.

"Being big doesn't mean you're never scared of stuff," Marsh replied.

Since Marsh wasn't the mystery dinosaur, Bill and his friends said goodbye and headed off to keep looking.

After walking for a little while, the four dinosaurs came across the entrance to the Cave of Shrieks. As they looked through the jagged rocks into the darkness, they could hear a deep, BOOMING voice coming from inside.

"Mystery dino, is that you?" Bill called.

"Could be-be-be . . ." came a loud echoing reply that sent rocks crumbling from the cave roof. Suddenly, something jumped out from the shadows . . .

"IGNATIUS?" cried the little dinos.

"But you're much too small to be the mystery dino!" said Bill.

"Actually, I don't mind being small," said Ignatius.

It's much easier to hide from Giganto!

"I wonder if I'll **EVER** find the mystery dino," Bill said. The four friends moved on to search along the beach by the lake.

Suddenly, a ripple spread across the water and a terrifyingly toothy head emerged.

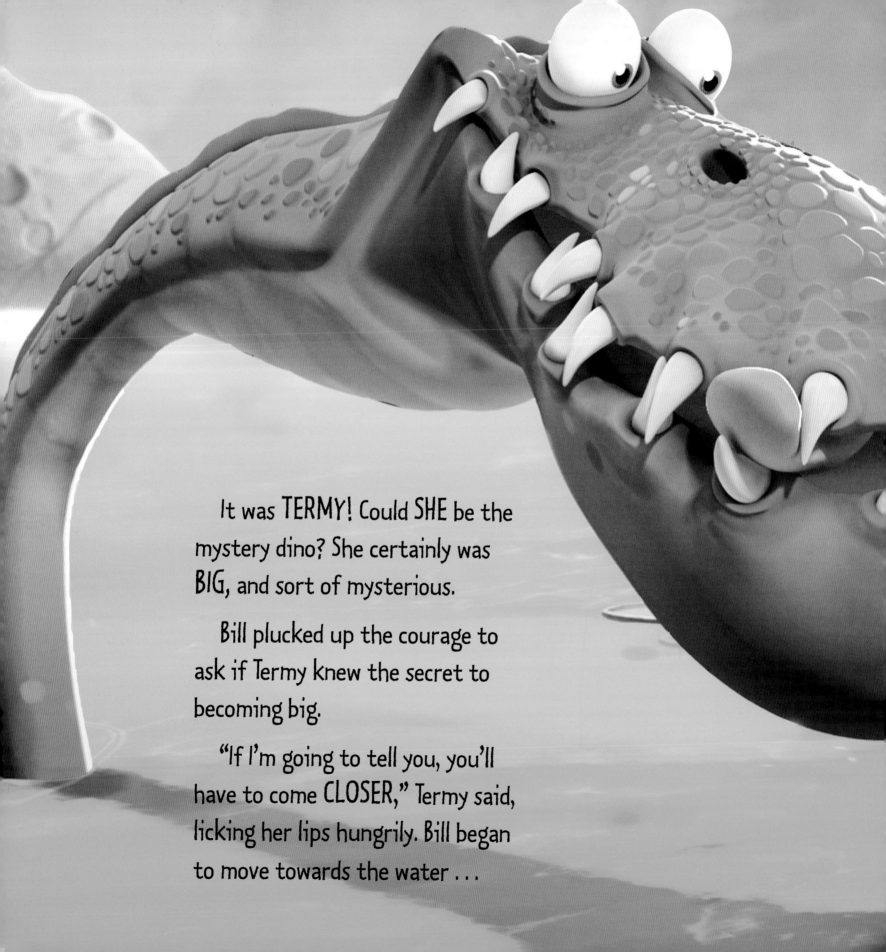

It was TERMY! Could SHE be the mystery dino? She certainly was BIG, and sort of mysterious.

Bill plucked up the courage to ask if Termy knew the secret to becoming big.

"If I'm going to tell you, you'll have to come CLOSER," Termy said, licking her lips hungrily. Bill began to move towards the water . . .

. . . but he suddenly stopped as he realised what Termy was doing. "Hey, you're just trying to trick me!" he said angrily. "I might have fallen for that when I was little, but not now!"

"There's no fooling you anymore, is there?" said Termy, looking down at Bill proudly. "My little blue yum-yum is all grown up!"

She wiped away a tear and plunged back into the water.

YOU'RE not the mystery dino!

"But I still have so much growing up to do," Bill said, feeling confused.

"Termy means that growing up isn't just about getting a bigger body. It's about growing in HERE," explained Mazu, pointing to her head.

"Yeah!" agreed Rocky. "And according to Iggy, bigger isn't always better."

"And Marsh said you can be big and STILL be afraid of stuff," added Tiny.

Bill was still sure that the mystery dino must know the real secret to becoming big. Perhaps they were hiding in the canyon.

What does it really mean to be BIG?

But when the dinos reached the top of the canyon and looked down, they were surprised to see . . .

GIGANTOSAURUS!

Bill stopped and thought. Could Giganto be the mystery dino? After all, he did know a thing or two about being big.

"Giganto IS mysterious," said Mazu, looking through her Gigantopedia. "There's so much to learn about him!"

Down in the canyon, Giganto stomped his foot on a rock, then walked away. Mazu spotted a strange shape where he'd been standing and pulled out her spyglass to get a better look.

Rocky, Bill and Tiny peered curiously over her shoulder, but they were still too far away to tell what they were looking at.

"I'm still not sure what it is," Mazu said. "Let's go and see!"

On closer inspection, Mazu realised that the shape was the latest in a long line of Giganto's footprints. They went from small to large – just like the marks on the little dinos' growth wall!

Bill placed his foot in Giganto's huge footprint. "I'm TINY compared to him," he groaned.

"Yes, but look at the smallest print," said Rocky, pointing to the first one. Carefully, Bill put his foot into the print. It fit!

Bill realised that Giganto must once have been as small as he was.

The little dinos raced back up the canyon to find Ayati. Bill couldn't wait to tell her everything he'd learned.

"I found out that bigger isn't always better, and you can be big but still be scared. Plus, you don't just grow on the outside – you grow in here, too!" he said, tapping his head. All of a sudden, Bill realised who the mystery dino was . . .

It's ME!

It's nice to meet you, mystery dino!

There was still the best secret of all to tell Ayati.

"Someday, I'LL be as big as Giganto," said Bill. "It's just going to take time."

With all his friends around him, Bill didn't mind waiting a little longer.

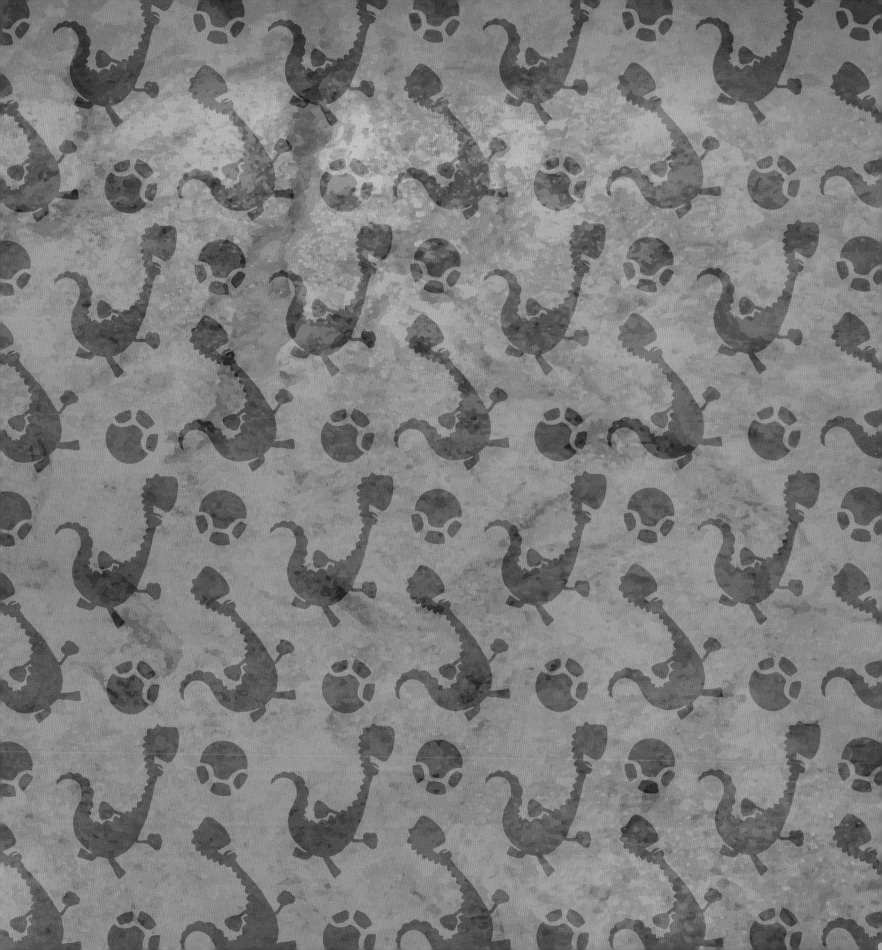

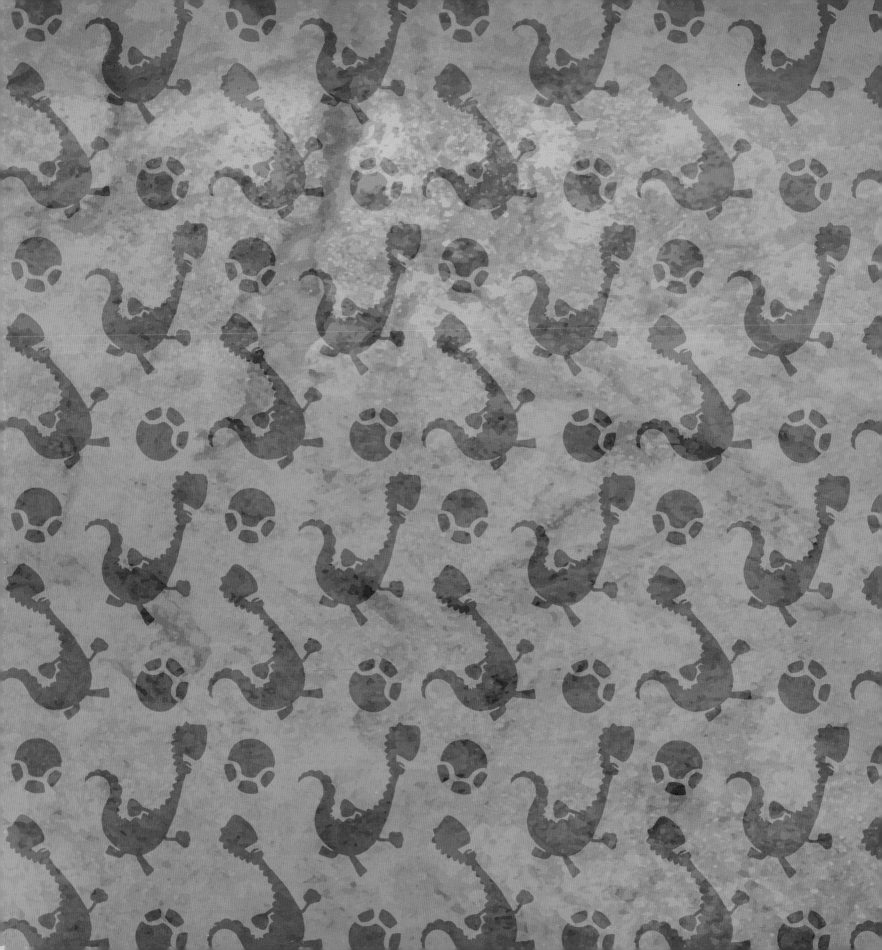